This time THEy Hear you

short stories by
BRIDGES PUBLIC CHARTER SCHOOL'S
THIRD GRADE CLASS

foreword by MINH LÊ

Published in May 2019
Copyright © 2019 826DC and the authors.
All rights reserved.

IBSN: 978-1-948644-30-3
Library of Congress Catalogue
Printed in the United States of America

First Edition

All proceeds from the sale of this book support 826DC's free writing programs.
Thank you for your support!

3333 14TH STREET NW, SUITE M120
WASHINGTON, DC 20010
202.525.1074 · WWW.826DC.ORG

826DC is a nonprofit organization dedicated to supporting students ages 6-18 with their creative and expository writing skills, and to helping teachers inspire their students to write. Our services are structured around our understanding that great leaps in learning can happen with one-on-one attention and that strong writing skills are fundamental to future success.

826DC Staff, School Year 2018-2019 • Zachary Clark, Executive Director • Areesah Mobley, Director of Development • Cedric Brown, Deputy Store Manager • D'Real Graham, Community Programs Manager • Cris Lee, In-School Programs Manager • Emily Moses, Publication Programs Manager • Sarah Richman, Development and Communications Manager • Shayna Baggatts-Porter, Special Projects Associate • Eileen Chong, After-School Writing Lab Coordinator • Kelsey McClure, Americorps Vista Volunteer Engagement Specialist • Brandi Shorts, Americorps Vista Development Systems Specialist

Author Photographs by Annie Wheeler
Design by Gigi Mascarenas

This time THEY Hear You

short stories by
BRIDGES PUBLIC CHARTER SCHOOL'S
Third Grade Class

foreword by MINH Lê

CONTENTS

FOREWORD

by Minh Lê

This year, citizens of Earth bid a teary farewell to "Oppy," an intrepid robot who spent the last 15 years sending detailed dispatches from the surface of Mars.

Even with the current onslaught of news, every now and then a certain story pokes its head out of the timeline and gives you pause. For me, that was the case with this 2019 headline about "Opportunity," NASA's interplanetary robot sending its last message from the Red Planet. I did a double take because my nine-year-old self would be rocked to his scrawny little core to know that this was news and not science fiction. If you had told me this in third grade, I would have bet you a pack of Now and Laters (my favorite candy) that you were reading to me from a sci-fi bestseller. Dispatches from Mars? Loveable robots with adorable nicknames? Those were exactly the kind of impossible dreams that kept my childhood imagination up, late into the night.

That's the wondrous thing about science fiction: with time, it can become reality. The science part is clear. The deep research and technical skill needed to achieve something like "Opportunity" is staggering. But the fiction side of this equation is where so much of the magic happens. Because first and foremost, for any real advance to be possible, we have to be able to look beyond the limits of our world. Long before we can launch robots onto the surface of another planet, we have to be able to

imagine and write absurd stories about it.

Which brings us to this book that you hold in your hands right now.

Yes, what you are holding is an exciting new collection of short fiction. Yes, it was written by some of the nimblest minds of a young generation. But it is also so much more. For within these pages are actual messages from The Future.

Of course, right now many of these tales will seem too far-fetched to ever become reality. But I'll wager good money (*and* a stale pack of Now and Laters) that we'll look back on *This Time They Hear You* and find it contains gems that proved to be quite prescient.

The question is: Which ones?

In twenty years, perhaps Brooklyn Michelle DeChabert will still be writing about Plymnastics (aka, Plant Gymnastics)—only in 2039 she'll be covering the Plymnastics Championships for the sports section of the *Washington Intergalactic Post.*

Or maybe in a few short years, households all over the world will be equipped with a Golden Matter, Josue Turcios Salmeron's evil robot who watches TV with you and cleans your house. This one is probably a solid bet because, truth be told, it feels like we already have one foot firmly planted in Golden Matter's universe. (Alexa: Look up "modern dystopian nightmare.")

And of course, the stories that do not turn out to become real are no less valuable. We may never encounter a talking willow tree like the one in Ursula Adeline Mahoney Dingee's story... but we can take her message of environmental stewardship to heart as we search for urgent solutions to climate change.

Indeed, creativity is the bridge that connects us to the innovations of the future. And, luckily for us, the young writers of 826DC are overflowing with the stuff.

So we don't need a multi-million dollar space robot to reveal what's lurking in the great unknown (no offense, Oppy). Not when right now, in our nation's capital, just a few miles away from NASA headquarters, hidden in an unassuming magic shop, this team of fearless writers is busy exploring the boundaries of fiction, challenging hardened literary tropes, and maybe even predicting the future, one impossible sentence at a time.

While these glittering stories are clearly reward enough, I also want to personally thank you for reading *This Time They Hear You*...because when it comes to investing in the future of young people and supporting their creative pursuits, there is no time like the present.

Minh Lê is an acclaimed children's author whose most recent picture book, *Drawn Together*, won the 2019 Asian/Pacific American Award for Literature. His other books include *Let Me Finish!* (an NPR Best Book of 2016), the upcoming *The Perfect Seat*, and *Green Lantern: Legacy*, a middle grade graphic novel coming in 2020 from DC Comics. In addition to books, he has written about children's literature for a variety of publications, including the New York Times, HuffPost, and NPR. Outside of spending time with his beautiful wife and sons in their home near Washington D.C., his favorite place to be is in the middle of a good book.

INTRODUCTION

by Emily Moses

So.

You're holding *This Time They Hear You* in your hands, and you either know what this book is, or you are about to find out what this book is.

You've heard from acclaimed author Minh Lê in the Foreword about the hope that erupts from this book, and you've seen the gorgeous cover and layout that the inimitable Gigi Mascarenas designed for us. Maybe you flipped through the interior, stopping to admire the splashy illustrations our team of nineteen professional artists created. Maybe you checked the back of the book and saw the dynamic author portraits local photographer Annie Wheeler shot, or read the deep gratefulness Kennerley Roper expressed on behalf of 826DC in the Acknowledgements. Perhaps you opened the book right to this Introduction (in which case, *hello*).

These things are all wonderful, hard-wrought, exciting elements to this book, yes. And don't get us wrong—we've spent the last year collecting all these necessary pieces because we believed it our responsibility to create the most lovely and impactful book possible.

The real reason we are all here, though, is for the fifty-six young authors whose stories burst from this book with such purity and urgency, we can no longer keep them to ourselves.

Take, for example, Hienos Tekeste's "Plant City," a story in which local superhero, PlantSaver, uses his celebrity for the greater good—most specifically, his environmentalist agenda.

Or, there's "The Problem That Has Been Solved." Though this may seem like your average, everyday story about daffodils that go to school, author Bemnet Lodebo sneaks in and teaches you a big lesson about the value of perseverance in the face of bullying.

There are forty-two stories in this book, each with their own merits. Ephratah Tsegaye's "The Man Who Stole the Seeds" is a story about poverty, resourcefulness, and, ultimately, generosity. Heran Zelalem's "Stinkey and the Rose" reminds you of the importance and beauty of finding friends who understand and support you, even if it is supporting you in being stinky.

Our young authors embraced the challenge of storytelling with such personality and gusto that we, as teachers, volunteers, and dedicated aides, couldn't help but honor the beautiful variety of work. You'll read "Mickey Bear and Natu the Dragon" by The Storytelling Squad, a crew of fourteen students who collaborated to write a single story, start to finish, together. You'll read a few stories that couldn't be contained in one part and therefore *needed* chapters, and you'll read "No Bullying" by Josiah French, a story so powerfully succinct, she was able to fit it into a comic strip.

As you turn the pages and enjoy *This Time They Hear You*, you're going to travel the full spectrum of emotion and experience—and, why wouldn't you? This book is an exploration, a celebration, and a promise, written by fifty-six authors who each carry their own perspective, their own stories, and their own voice. It is an honor, then, to introduce you to the thoughtful and hardworking third graders from Bridges Public Charter School, and to their stories.

Without further ado, my friends, welcome to *This Time They Hear You.*

MICKEY BEAR AND NATU THE DRAGON

written by The Storytelling Squad
illustrated by Max Reinhard

Once upon a time, there was a brown bear named Mickey Bear. He lived in a dark tunnel inside a mountain. Mickey Bear had a very fun time with his life. He had very short brown hair and always wore a special red baseball hat because he was a baseball coach.

He liked playing baseball with his three brothers, Mike, Daniel, and James. One day, they went to play baseball at the bear playground on the mountain.

Then...he came out of nowhere! Natu the dragon flew by and took their ball.

They did not know who the dragon was at first, so they were scared when Natu took the ball. Then they saw Natu's red scales and shark teeth and knew it was him.

"Hey, can I have my ball back?" yelled Mickey Bear.

Then, Mickey Bear and his brother started being friends with the dragon because he was sharing the ball and being nice. They were all happy, and went to Chuck E. Cheese together. (The dragon's dad took them.)

Then, they all had a sleepover. The End.

Mathias Beard is a fun and funny eight-year-old who loves to play. In his free time, he likes watching videos and reading comic books. He's very athletic. His favorite sports include baseball, soccer, tennis, and lacrosse. His favorite part of school is playing in PE, going to recess, and playing on the computer.

Josiah Eury is eight years old. His hobbies include going to birthday parties and going places with his grandma and cousins. At school, he likes recess the most. Basketball is Josiah's favorite sport. When he grows up he'd like to be a traffic man.

Micah Eury is happy on cloudy days. He likes dinosaurs, music, and television. He also likes to play outside. He prefers popcorn and oranges.

Tomas Fita is a fun and energetic student. He loves to run and play sports. He is a great helper to all teachers and loves to lend a hand whenever he can.

Lauren Goganious enjoys playing outside on sunny days. She likes to exercise. She also loves to play with blocks. Some foods she prefers are popcorn and oranges. Lauren also likes to watch TV.

Akhil Hart loves hugs, apples, and classical music. His favorite activities include puzzles and constructing/deconstructing things. Akhil's favorite color is green.

Jakobe Jones is really into fashion and modeling. In his free time, he loves shopping for new clothes. He always looks stylish at school. Jakobe also loves to draw.

Joe'L Lawrence is a dancer. Watch out for his slick dance moves! He also loves drawing and making things. He enjoys sports, including basketball and football. He likes the LEGO Ninjago books and movies, as well as *PJ Masks*. When he grows up, he'd like to be a basketball player or a police officer.

Kayden Lee prefers a nice, sunny day to a cloudy one. He likes toys, like action heroes. He also likes to play outside and watch TV. He enjoys apples and popcorn.

Bryson McCoy is a big fan of Mickey Mouse books and movies. He also loves eating Goldfish crackers. Bryson is very friendly to all students and staff, and he loves hugs.

Marcus Novoa is a hip guy who loves drawing and reading. *Pete the Cat* is his favorite book series. He also likes *The LEGO Movie*. Marcus is interested in sports, including soccer and football. When he grows up he'd like to be an American football player.

Tyler Stewart loves to see the sun shining through the window as he plays inside. He enjoys toy action heroes and watching TV. He also likes to draw. Tyler likes to eat oranges and fruit snacks.

Cameron Wise is a third grader. She loves nursery rhymes and having stories read to her. She also enjoys interacting with her iPad.

PINE AND WILLOW WITH THE BULLIES

written by Sebastian Stone Perea
illustrated by Leslie Osmont

In the beginning, there was a little tree called Willow. He lived in a park near a little pond with other trees. One day, the trees started picking on him because he was different.

One of the trees said, "Why are you sad?"

Willow said, "Because you are teasing me."

There was another tree named Pine. Pine looked like a Christmas tree. The other trees also teased Pine because he was the only pine tree.

The other trees said, "Hey Pine! Why do you look like a Christmas tree?"

Pine said, "That's because I am a Christmas tree."

The other trees said, "Of course you are! That's why you are different, and we're smarter than you."

So when Pine grew up, he saw Willow getting bullied.

Then Pine said, "STOP!"

The other tree said, "What are you going to do?"

So Willow said, "You heard him, stop!"

And so Pine and Willow became friends, because Willow saved Pine from being teased and Pine saved Willow from being teased.

The End.

One thing about Sebastian Stone Perea is that sometimes he talks too much. He is kind. Sebastian's teachers are Ms. Childs, Ms. Reese, and Ms. Jenny. He is smart and likes PE.

The Cacti and the Goats

written by Jervon Watson
illustrated by Patricia Baca

Once upon a time, the cacti lived peacefully. Then the goats came.

The cacti's names were Cuco, Spike, and Jerry. The goats stole all of their things, so the cacti and the goats were feuding.

Later on, when they had stopped feuding, one of the goats snuck and took the cacti's resources while the others weren't paying attention.

The cacti and the goats decided to race to decide who gets to keep the cacti's things.

Cuco, Jerry, and Spike are cacti, so they have roots and can't race.

....

Jervon Watson is a person from Washington, DC. He likes pie, Six Flags, *Pokémon*, *Yu-Gi-Oh!*, *Digimon*, and books. He also likes video games and board games. He is good at math.

The Forest

written by Marjorie Valladares-Vera
illustrated by Caitlin Saharek

This story is about Jimmy and me, Marjorie.

Jimmy was a tree and he wanted to be my friend. To be my friend, Jimmy thought he had to be a person because I am a person.

The problem was people were bullying him and that made him sad. No one was giving him water. He did not want to be a person anymore because he saw that people can be mean.

Jimmy said to the bullies, "Stop! I don't like it!"

So the bullies stopped and said they were sorry, and we are all friends now.

Marjorie Valladares-Vera is a girl from Washington, DC. She likes to eat fruit. She is so smart, and she likes balloons. When she gets older, she is going to put fruit on the wall.

THE CANDY RACE!

written by Manea Oulare
illustrated by Samantha Lane Fiddy

Sugarville is having a candy race! A candy race is a race with candy cars, and it's only for mean kids.

Chloe cannot participate in the race because Chloe is not mean.

Taffy is mean to Chloe, and she is a girl. Her mom and dad are mean, too!

King Candy is the King of Sugarville. He can decide to let Chloe into the candy race. Chloe makes candy for King Candy and Taffy. They became nice because the candy has a reverse potion that makes mean people nice.

King Candy said, "You can be in the race!" It was a close race. Chloe won the race. The End.

Manea Oulare's favorite thing to do is go to school. She is eight, and her birthday is on April 25th. She has a birthday twin named Sofia. Manea is going to be nine in two months.

Ninja/Nick

written by Anna Flowers
illustrated by Santiago Casares

CHAPTER 1: THE WOODS

One day, Ninja wanted to take his plant named Nick with him to Lake City.

Ninja said, "Nick, if you see someone trying to cut down a tree—Nick!—you better tell me so I can stop them. So, are you ready, Nick?"

"Yeah!" said Nick.

"Okay! Let's go!" said Ninja.

"But Ninja, how are we going?" said Nick.

"Oh, I didn't tell you? We are taking an Uber."

CHAPTER 2: THE UBER

"Let's go, man. He should be here!" said Ninja.

"Oh, is that him?"

"Yeah, it is him. Hi, Uber Man!" said Nick and Ninja.

"Oh hi. So where are we going, Nag-na?" the Uber Man asked.

"No! It's Ninja!" said Ninja.

"Ooooooh Ninja...so Ninja where am I taking you?" asked the Uber Man.

"We are going to Lake City!" said Nick and Ninja.

"Oh! I thought it was Lick City." said Uber Man.

"No! LAKE CITY," said Ninja and Nick.

One hour later: "...Hey we're here. Thank you!" said Nick and Ninja.

CHAPTER 3

"Hey Ninja?"

"Yeah, Nick?" said Ninja.

"I'm scared."

"Why, Nick? Look at all the trees! What is scary about them?"

"GRRRRRRRRRRR!"

"Huh? What?" Nick and Ninja didn't know what was growling.

"Hey, if you want to take a photo, you have to give us something first," said the trees.

"How about some water? Do you need sunlight?" Nick asked. Nick and Ninja gave the trees water, and they were allowed to take a photo.

Nick and Ninja left without any parts of their body missing. The End.

....

Anna "A.C." Flowers was born on June 19. Her favorite game is *Fortnite*. When Anna was a baby, she hated water. She also loves playing sports.

Plants and Camels Having Fun

written by Malik Damar Blackwell
illustrated by Halsey Berryman

This story takes place in a jungle oasis in a desert. Ricky is a cactus and Timothy is a thorny rose. Timothy and Ricky are playing around, having fun, talking, and laughing.

Eli and Liam are twin camel brothers. Every day, they come over and eat parts of Ricky and Timothy. Timothy and Ricky feel bad because the camels eat them and it hurts! They are sad and scared.

Ricky and Timothy come up with a solution. Timothy decides to use his thorns to make one camel stop, and Ricky decides to use his spikes to make the other camel stop.

They poke the camels. The thorns

Malik Damar Blackwell is a Virgo. His favorite color is yellow. He likes going to SkyZone and Dave & Buster's. His favorite thing to do is jump on trampolines.

and spikes hurt their gums, so the camels walk away and leave them alone.

But suddenly Timothy and Ricky change their minds.

They say excitedly, "Wait! Wait! Come back! We want to pull the spikes and thorns out!"

Then they all have fun, make jokes, and live happily ever after.

THE WIZARD OF SUGARVILLE

written by Kaliyah Howard
illustrated by Christina Girardi

Once upon a time, there was a little girl named Princess Bella. Bella was eating her favorite royal soup when a tornado came, and she got sucked up. When she woke up, she was in Sugarville!

Bella was lost, so she walked until she saw someone: the Wicked Witch! Bella went to the Wicked Witch and she gave Bella some red shoes with glitter.

"Thank you, these shoes are beautiful," Bella said. "What's your name?"

The Wicked Witch disappeared without answering, so Bella just walked off.

A Scarecrow named Princess Emma saw Bella and said, "Hey! Hey! Hey!"

That got Bella's attention. Bella said, "Yes?"

Emma said, "Come here."

"Ok," Bella said. "AAAaaaHHHhhh! You...you are a talking scarecrow! I am leaving!"

"No, wait!" Emma said. "Can you help me?"

"With what?"

"I want a brain. I want to be smart like you!" said Emma.

"Okay," Bella said. "Let me help. My name is Princess Bella and I am going to The Wonderful Wizard of Sugarville so I can go back home. I will bring you, and you can ask for a brain."

"Thanks, Bella," said Princess Emma. So they walked and, when they were in the woods, the Wicked Witch came back and followed Bella and Emma. While she was following them, she whispered nice things to trick them.

Emma said, "Wait, someone is following us. I think it is the Wicked Witch, but she's being nice... don't listen! It is a TRAP! She is going to get you!"

"Look, there is a pond," said Princess Bella.

"Yeah, let's put water on the Wicked Witch so she will melt," said Princess Emma. She knew how to make the Wicked Witch go away because she was originally from Sugarville.

"Got ya!" Bella and Emma said as they tossed water at the Wicked Witch.

"AAAaaaHHHhhh! I am melt...melt...melting..." And the Wicked Witch disappeared.

"Yay, we got her! Let's go," said Princess Bella.

They started walking again until they heard, "Hello, hello!"

"Who is that?" asked Emma.

"I do not know...AAAaaaHHHhhh! You are a talking lion! Don't eat me!" Bella yelled. But when she did, she scared the talking lion.

"Bella, give her a chance like you did for me, okay?" said Emma.

"Okay," said Bella.

"Can you help me? I want some more courage," said the lion.

"We can help! We are going to the Wonderful Wizard of Sugarville," said Emma.

"Okay, let's go!" said the lion.

So they walked and walked.

"Hey, hey, who's that?" asked Bella.

"Nobody," said a tin woman.

"Who said that?" asked Emma.

"Shassa. Princess Shassa," said the tin woman.

"Great name...AAAaaaHHHhhh! You're...

you're a talking tin woman!" said Bella.

Bella decided to give Princess Shassa a chance like she gave the others.

"Fine, what do you need?" asked Bella.

"I want a better heart so I can be healthy like you," said Princess Shassa.

A note came from the sky and fell on Bella's nose. "Hum, what's this?"

"Before you read me, what's your name?" the note said.

"My name is Princess Bella. What's yours?"

"Kaliyah. Princess Kaliyah," said the note.

"Wow, a lot of princesses like me! Yay! So, what do you say, Princess Kaliyah?" asked Bella.

The note responded, "Come to the tower right now."

"Where is the tower?" asked Princess Emma, the lion, and Princess Shassa.

"Ooh, there it is! Look up!" said Princess Bella.

"That is super tall. Let's go!"

When they got to the tower, there were so many stairs there. Like, one billion stairs. So much drama.

After a long time, they were done walking up the stairs. They asked the Wonderful Wizard of Sugarville for the things they wanted, and everyone got what they wanted.

The End.

....

Kaliyah Howard is nine. Her birthday is February 27, and her favorite hobbies are modeling, dance, and acting. Her first favorite inspiration is Tyra Banks, and her second favorite inspiration is Naomi Campbell. Her favorite book is *Nothing's Fair in Fifth Grade* by Barthe DeClements. Kaliyah's favorite subjects are reading and math because they are fun to her. What Kaliyah wants to be when she grows up is a model and fashion designer. Kaliyah has two sisters and one dad and one mom. This is Kaliyah's author biography.

NO BULLYING

written by Josiah French
illustrated by George Nichols IV

The bully said, "I don't like your tree. It looks ugly. I'm going to put mud on it, and I'm going to spit on it.

I'm going to block the sunlight from your tree. Your tree is so, so dumb."

Josiah said, "No, its not!

I'm wiping your spit from my tree. I'm giving it sunlight, and I'm going to put water back on it."

Josiah "Jojo" French lives in Washington, DC. Her favorite book is *How the Grinch Stole Christmas!* Her favorite thing to do is cartwheels, and 14 people in her family like to copy her movements. Her family is the best family ever.

ROSE AND ALL THE PLANTS

written by Genesis Fuentes-Ramirez
illustrated by Sid Champagne

PART 1

Rose and Daisy had so much light in their greenhouse that, if they didn't move, Rose and Daisy would bloom the next day! Until a new plant came in. The owner of the greenhouse moved Rose and Daisy to make room. Both were very cold in their new spot. After two hours without sun, they couldn't bloom. They needed sun.

Then, the greenhouse owner came and saw how sad the plants were, so she decided to move the new plant. (The new plant also was sad when the new plant was put in the sunlight because the new plant didn't need a lot of sunlight.) It was a happy solution.

PART 2

Rose and Daisy were not in the greenhouse, just outside in the hot weather. Then, a darkness spread.

Then Rose said, "A solar eclipse!

"Oh no!" Daisy shouted.

PART 3

On May 30th, Rose and Daisy were sitting by bay. They drank the water and both ate sunlight. Yum, they slurped the meal!

But something was happening. Rumble...earthquake...rumble!

"Are we going to die?"

"What!? You are insane!" said Rose. "Stop and think it through!"

So they thought. Rose had an idea while it was rumbling, and she said, "We can get shelter!" So they got shelter and the earthquake stopped.

Genesis Fuentes-Ramirez is a student. She is almost nine years old. She lives in Washington, DC. Her teachers are Ms. Childs, Ms. Jenny, Ms. Reese, and Mr. Kevin. Her favorite month is June.

VILLAINS VS. HEROES

written by Sierra Amber Howard
illustrated by Teresa Roberts Logan

Once upon a time in Florida, there were two heroes: V and Rap Monster. V was a boy with the power to teleport. V was very tall and buff and skinny with black hair and a normal face. Rap Monster was a boy with the power to turn into a monster—any monster, you name it! Rap Monster was skinny with black hair.

One day, while watching their security cameras, they saw Jimin and Sierra stealing people's money and gold. So V and Rap Monster went to stop them. The city they lived in was supposed to be nice and they wanted it to stay the way it was, not get worse.

Jimin had purple hair, but he liked to dye it. He had ice powers, which he used to freeze people so he could take their money. Jimin also distracted people by pointing and saying, "Look, a snake!" and stealing when people looked away.

Sierra also had purple hair and also had a lot of powers: the power to teleport, turn into a monster, and freeze people.

V teleported to Jimin and Sierra. Jimin saw V and morphed into Rap Monster to trick V, because Rap Monster was trapped in a cage. While V and Jimin were at the police station, Rap Monster and Sierra were in the cage. And then Sierra realized she had a crush on Jimin.

Sythel, Queen of Florida, visited them in jail and they told her their story. They told Queen Sythel they stole the money to go back to their home, Mic City. The Queen felt mercy and told the police they're innocent and to let them go.

Then Sierra told Jimin that she liked him. Jimin liked Sierra. They became boyfriend and girlfriend.

And they lived happily ever after. The End.

....

Sierra Amber Howard lives in Washington, DC. She is eight years old. She likes eating ice cream. She loves Disney. Her favorite sport is tennis. She wants to be royal, like the Queen of England.

They Live in the Clouds

written by Ariel Rodriguez Beltran
illustrated by Leslie Osmont

Once upon a time, there was a boy named Jake Paul who lived in Cloud City. Jake had brothers named The Mean Boys. Their mom picked them up from Cloud School and then they went home.

On the way home from Cloud School, The Mean Boys pushed Jake Paul out of Cloud City. Jake fell for one hour. He landed on a bank.

His friend Joe's house was on Earth, so he went to his friend's house. He knocked on the door but no one answered, so he rang to doorbell. Joe's mom answered the door.

"I'm so cold," Jake said.

Joe's mom said, "Come in, come in. I'll give you some hot chocolate." Then she said, "Son, come down, your friend is here."

In the clouds, Jake Paul's mom said, "Mean Boys, where's my other kid, Jake Paul? I'm going to Earth to look for my kid."

The mom jumped to Earth with a parachute. She landed on a bank, just like Jake did. And then the mom put signs everywhere that said,

"Have you seen my kid? Are you looking for my kid? Please please please please!"

Jake went to talk to Joe and asked, "Do you have a rocket to take me back to Cloud City?"

Joe said, "Yes, it's outside. Let's go now."

And Jake said, "Let's go."

Joe gave Jake Paul a rocketship so he could go home.

Meanwhile, Jake Paul's mom remembered and said, "His friend Joe's house on Earth! I'll go to his friend's house." She knocked on Joe's door but no one answered. Then she rang the doorbell and someone answered. It was Joe's mom.

Jake's mom said, "Where is my kid?"

Joe's mom said, "Go to the kitchen, and then go through the door. They're in the backyard."

Jake's mom went to the backyard and said, "Wait! Jake Paul, wait!" and Jake Paul's mom ran as fast as she could.

Yes! She got into the rocketship just in time and flew home with Jake to Cloud City.

Ariel Rodriquez Beltran is a young author from Washington, DC. He likes to go to the movies. He likes pets and playing games. *Grand Theft Auto V* and *Fortnite* are his favorite to play. One day, he wants to own a Ferrari and a Lamborghini.

TOTAL DRAMA-RAMA

written by Destinee Jones
illustrated by Santiago Casares

Once upon a time, there were four plants named Emma, Ziri, Marcelyne, and Tiffiny. Tiffiny used to be a nice girl, but she was forced to become a bully by her control freak and bully friend, Marcelyne.

Emma, she was shy and sweet—like, the sweetest thing in the world—but that doesn't mean she wasn't bullied by…gulp… Marcelyne! Emma was a huge corpse flower. She smelled like the sweetest candy in the world, like caramel and chocolate mixed together. Emma had blonde hair coming out of the back of her flower. Ziri is Emma's sister and best friend, except she has curly brown hair and she smells like a daisy flower.

Marcelyne looked like a violet, and she thought she was the beautifulest, sassiest, best flower at school. She would flip her petals in everyone's face and everyone talked about her behind her back, but sometimes Emma and Ziri thought she deserved it because Marcelyne always pushed Emma and Ziri to the ground and threatened them.

One day, Emma was getting ready for school when she heard a whirring sound. She thought it was a headache, but really it was a vision! In the vision, she saw Marcelyne getting dragged into detention by a teacher.

"Maybe I should go into the bathroom and put water on my face," Emma thought.

That same day, Marcelyne came up to Emma and Ziri and, right as a teacher walked by, threw herself on the ground and began to fake cry.

"Two hours of DETENTION for you!" the teacher said to Emma and Ziri.

Emma and Ziri said, "No! That is not fair. We don't like this idea!"

Marcelyne grumbled and rumbled.

Emma and Ziri told the teacher what happened, and the teacher grabbed Marcelyne and dragged her into detention instead.

After that, Marcelyne didn't bully Emma and Ziri, Tiffiny was nice to them again, and they all lived happily ever after.

Destinee Jones is nine years old. She likes to play *Minecraft* with her cousins. Her other hobby is playing football. Her favorite books are about Pete the Cat. Her favorite movie is *Delhi Safari*. Her favorite sport is football. She lives with her sister, brothers, and their friends. She wants to be a singer when she grows up, like Rihanna.

The Spiky Cactus

written by Jayden Trice
illustrated by Kendall Ladd

Hi, my name is Scratchy! I am a cactus, and I have no hands.

I have no friends because I am too spiky. I used to have friends but, when they got too close to me, I accidentally hurt them with my spikes. It also happened when people try to take a picture with me. If people try to climb me, they will get spiked.

I decided to cut off my spikes and grow arms. And then I went to a party. I made new friends, and didn't hurt them because I cut off my spikes. My friends and I took some pictures together.

Jayden Trice loves to play his Xbox One. He also likes to football, basketball, and watch YouTube. His favorite snack is Flamin' Hot Cheetos. Jayden loves to play *NBA 2K19* on his Xbox One. He currently lives in Washington, DC. His birthday is February 20.

Three Little Pigs in DC

written by Wuan Shields
illustrated by Julia Gualtieri

There once were three little pigs named Jordan, Morgan, and Jayden. They were hungry, so they went to the store.

The pigs saw their friend Wuan on the walk. Wuan was wearing Vans shoes, black pants, a black shirt, and a Jason Voorhees Part 6 hockey mask. He said, "Hi."

Wuan and the pigs were in the store, but so was a gray wolf. The wolf tried to hurt the pigs because he was hungry and didn't like the food in the store. The store was a Lunchables and cereal store that also had candy (and everything is free).

Wuan threw one of his shoes close to the wolf to scare him. The wolf ran away.

Wuan and the pigs got the dark blue Lunchables, chocolate Fruity Pebbles, and Hershey's and Reese's. Then they went home and ate, and they all lived happily after ever.

Wuan Shields was born November 5 in Washington, DC. He has a big brother. His favorite thing to do is play video games. His role model is his mom.

Jack and the Two Bullies

written by Landon Slade
illustrated by Samantha Lane Fiddy

In Tampa, Florida, there was daffodil named Jack.

He was playing with his friend at his friend's house. A few minutes later, Jack's friend's parents called them for lunch: two minutes!

Later, two storm clouds that were bullies came over and started to bully Jack. His friends came and saw that Jack was getting bullied, so they started to tell them to stop bullying Jack. But the two storm clouds started to rain on them and wouldn't stop! The two storm clouds rained on them for twenty minutes. Soon, Jack and his friends' roots started to flood, and they started to get worried about dying out.

The next day, it was the first day of summer so Dan the sun was out. Dan saw the two storm clouds, bigger than ever, going toward Jack and his friend, who were playing outside to get dry from yesterday's rain bullying.

When Jack's friend saw how big the storm clouds were, he and Jack started to hide so they wouldn't get rained on. But the two clouds found them because they're so big!

They had just started to rain on the daffodils when Dan the sun saw what the two huge storm clouds were doing, so Dan shined down on them so they couldn't rain on the daffodils anymore. Then, a palm tree started to lean over on top of Jack and his friend so they could dry.

A few hours later, when they were dried, Jack and his friend thanked the sun and the palm tree. They went home, ate lunch, went back outside, and played and played until they were called to bed. When they were outside the next day, they thought those two storm clouds would be outside, but they weren't! So Jack and his friends never saw the storm cloud bullies again.

Landon Slade is from Washington, DC. He is hyper, loves to play *Fortnite* and *Apex Legends*, and loves cake. Landon's birthday is March 11, 2010. He does not like to read a lot.

It's Time to Fight the Cowboys

written by Jehison Hernandez-Canales
illustrated by Halsey Berryman

Sam and the Candy People were happy in their candy village.

But one day, some cowboys came to take the village because of the Candy Trees. The Candy People were scared.

Some of the Candy People decided to fight back. They were hiding in the bushes to surprise them. They jumped out and started to spray candy on the cowboys so they would get sticky and have to leave.

The Candy People were stronger and the cowboys ran away. Sam and the Candy People were happy again.

Jehison Hernandez-Canales is a nine-year-old from Washington, DC. His favorite movie is *Bumblebee*. Football is one of his favorite sports. He likes watching YouTube, especially Jelly—the channel, not the food. He has one sister and one brother.

THE FIRE

written by Emmanuel Fuentes-Ardon
illustrated by Samantha Lane Fiddy

Once upon time, a Redwood tree lived happily in California. His name was Max, and he was twenty-five years old. He could talk with his Redwood friends. Their bark was rough. They mostly felt safe, and that's what mattered to Max.

One day it was Max's birthday! He and the rest of the Redwood trees celebrated. They ate original-flavored cake! Max's birthday wish was to be safe from danger.

That is what he wished.

But this happened: After ten years, there was a fire. He warned everybody in the forest but he couldn't run because of his roots! He was scared and worried.

Then, just when the fire was close, it rained!
Max said, "God saved us."

After it rained, all the Redwoods lived happily ever after!

Emmanuel Fuentes-Ardon is a gamer and vlogger. He is also a YouTuber. He has 29 videos. He has 16 subscribers. He is eight years old. He has an Xbox 360.

THE THREE FLOWERS

written by Genesis Perez Salvador
illustrated by Max Reinhard

This is the big friendly flower. Her name is Joy. Joy is with her brother, Sam. Her sister is called Friendly. All the flowers love and need the sun because without the sun the flowers die. And they also love rain because without rain they die.

They live on the planet Earth. The garden where they live has a star on top, but there is no sun and no rain. Also, there are some magic cones that grant wishes.

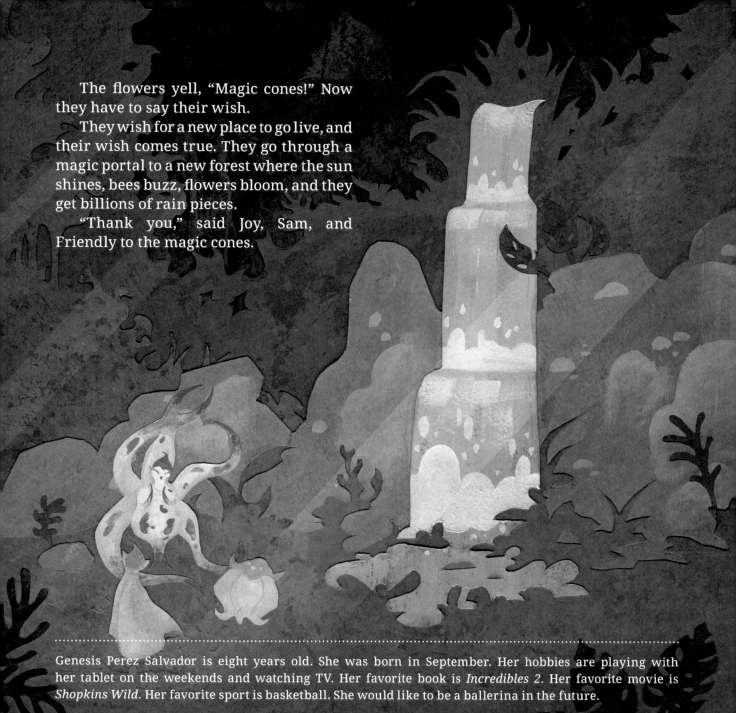

The flowers yell, "Magic cones!" Now they have to say their wish.

They wish for a new place to go live, and their wish comes true. They go through a magic portal to a new forest where the sun shines, bees buzz, flowers bloom, and they get billions of rain pieces.

"Thank you," said Joy, Sam, and Friendly to the magic cones.

Genesis Perez Salvador is eight years old. She was born in September. Her hobbies are playing with her tablet on the weekends and watching TV. Her favorite book is *Incredibles 2*. Her favorite movie is *Shopkins Wild*. Her favorite sport is basketball. She would like to be a ballerina in the future.

The World's Plymnastics Champs and How it All Happened

written by Brooklyn Michelle DeChabert
illustrated by Gigi Mascarenas

Far, far away, on a moon where people might someday live, Sofia Lorado Vance and her siblings, Brandin, Brooklyn, Landon, Latrice, and King, lived without their parents. Their mother and father died in an accident—a human took them out of the dirt and ate them because Sofia's parents were plants.

Sofia was like any regular old person, but she was a plant, too. She ate soil, water, compost, and sunlight. But she didn't really drink much water because she disliked water. She needed carbon dioxide or else she wouldn't be able to perform as a plymnast (a plant gymnast).

Her dream was to become a plymnastics champ, so she had to get to Earth for the World's Plymnastics Championships. She decided to take a meteor to Earth, but it crashed.

Luckily, someone saved Sofia! And it just so happened to be that the person who saved her was a retired plymnastics coach. The coach took Sofia to the tournament.

When it was her turn, Sofia Lorado Vance trembled. Then she got onto her stems and flipped up, over, and did an amazing forward kickover.

The judges narrated, "She places her stem on the mat. Now it is time for the backward kickover."

Her heart beat. There she was.

She kicked backwards over her head, but she didn't land the kickover. The crowd gasped.

But!

She did a full twist. No one in plymnastics history had ever done one before! The crowd went wild.

Sofia Lorado Vance won the World's Plymnastics Championships, and became a plymnastic champ. The End.

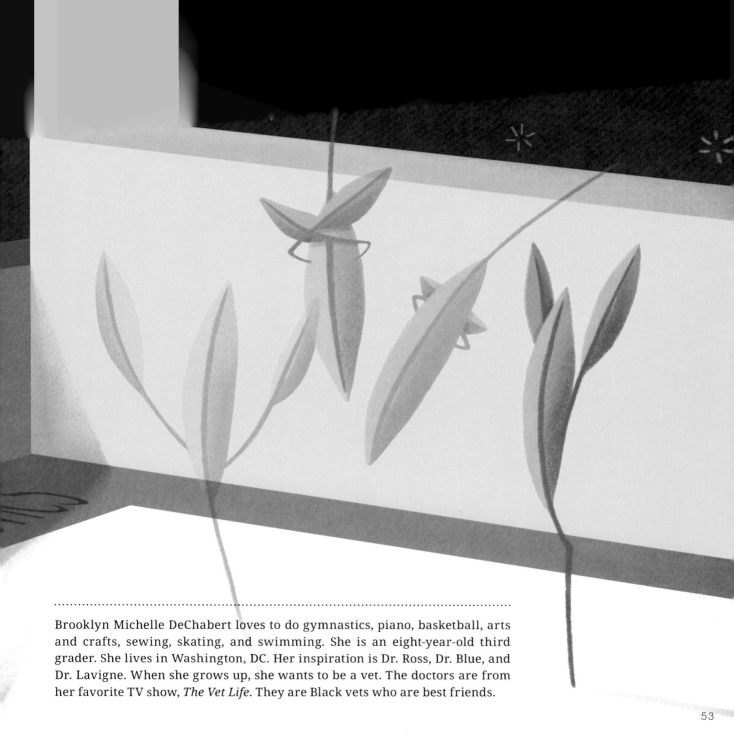

Brooklyn Michelle DeChabert loves to do gymnastics, piano, basketball, arts and crafts, sewing, skating, and swimming. She is an eight-year-old third grader. She lives in Washington, DC. Her inspiration is Dr. Ross, Dr. Blue, and Dr. Lavigne. When she grows up, she wants to be a vet. The doctors are from her favorite TV show, *The Vet Life*. They are Black vets who are best friends.

THE POTION

written by Angel Quinde Torres
illustrated by George Nichols IV

A long time ago, Jack lived in the woods. Jack walked all over the woods. As a human, he wanted to be a plant, so Jack went to the potion store and asked Rose for a plant potion.

Rose said, "I don't have a plant potion, but I can make one."

Jack stared. He said, "How long will it take?"

"A long time," said Rose.

Jack left the store and waited a long time. When the potion was ready, Jack took it. Little did he know, Jack turned into a corpse flower and he stunk.

As a corpse flower, Jack wanted to be human.

To be continued...

Angel Quinde Torres is a student at Bridges. He is from Washington, DC. He is nice. He is also cool.

The Best Garfield Runaway

written by Josue Turcios-Salmeron
illustrated by Patricia Baca

When Garfield got home from a sleepover at my house, he found out his toy, Golden Matter, was missing. Golden Matter was an evil robot toy with red eyes and one ear with wires, and his job was to help clean the house and watch TV with Garfield.

Garfield looked everywhere, and some other people also tried to look for Golden Matter, too.

Then he saw someone's dog with Golden Matter! The dog tried to scare Garfield, and Garfield tried to scare the dog with his sharp nails, some bigger than your head! The dog started barking and wanted to bite him.

Then the dog tried to fight Garfield. Garfield went inside and took a chair from the house. Garfield went up and then down the stairs.

Josue Turcios-Salmeron loves to play *Fortnite*. He also did the Cizzorz Death Run. He also loves to sleep, drink, eat, play with his friends, go to his cousin's house, go outside, and go to school. He also loves to play at the playground.

When Garfield got downstairs, he decided he was too tired to fight. They were going to fight each other, but they ran out of breath and were tired and decided to call a truce.

So, all three of them—the dog, Garfield, and Golden Matter—called a truce so they could be friends. They changed their minds about each other because they all looked cool, liked cool things, and had cool hair. Robots can also have hair.

The Man Who Stole the Seeds

written by Ephratah Tsegaye
illustrated by Kendall Ladd

Once upon a time, in 1918 in a land far away, there was a poor guy who was fired from his workplace five times. The last time he was fired, they took all of his money away.

He only had enough money to visit the jungle once. In the jungle, he found a giant plant with a lot of seeds, so he started stealing the seeds.

After a minute, the plant woke up and asked, "Why are you stealing my seeds?"

"So I can get a house," said the guy. "I don't have any money."

"Ok," said the plant, "I want to help you, but I need water."

The guy went looking for something to fill with water. The plant said, "I don't mind if you use your shoe." Then the guy left and filled his shoe with water to throw on the plant and the plant gave him lots of seeds.

They both lived happily ever after.

Ephratah Tsegaye is nine years old. Her favorite sport is tennis and when she grows up she wants to be a runner.

FRIENDS

written by Chase Brown

illustrated by Leslie Osmont

Chase and Mr. Kevin were coconut trees who met at Tree School. Tree School was in a jungle. Going to Tree School was fun, but the work was boring. Chase did not like doing all the work his tree teacher gave him.

Chase and Mr. Kevin liked to snack and play video games together. They were friends for three years.

Chase and Mr. Kevin wanted more tree friends because they were lonely. They wanted friends to play video games with. They also wanted a million dollars.

One time there was this bully at Tree School, and the bully said, "Which one of you is Mr. Kevin?"

Chase said, "I am Mr. Kevin!"

The bully said, "Ha! Let's see you try to beat me in a video game."

When the video game started, Chase started to win.

Then, he started to lose until he lost. Mr. Kevin was watching. When Chase lost, Mr. Kevin ran away. Chase felt angry about that.

Chase kept playing video games, and then he started bullying people, too. Mr. Kevin still didn't come back, this time because Chase was being a bully.

Chase stayed a bully until the first bully came back. They had a video game rematch. Chase started winning, then Chase started losing. The bully was winning, then the bully was losing.

In the end, Chase won.

Mr. Kevin came back because he heard that Chase won. When he got back, Chase was not a bully anymore. They felt happy because they had a stronger friendship now.

....

Chase Brown is eight years old, and he likes drawing. Chase likes books. He thinks he is cool. His favorite color is dark blue. His favorite book character is Dog Man.

FESCAPE

written by Samuel Medina
illustrated by Caitlin Cali

Alien is a half-eagle, half-horse that eats other birds and pops up in a bunch of my stories and, since he is hungry, he wants to eat Falcon.

Falcon is a friendly bird who is friends with Lightning, the quickest cheetah in NikeWorld, a medium-sized shoe where all these animals live.

Lightning loves to race around, and he is a good jumper.

When Falcon alerts Cheetah that Falcon is in danger, Cheetah wants to help Falcon but he doesn't know how. Falcon wants to escape from Alien, but he doesn't know how. He could escape out the shoelace of NikeWorld, or stay home and get destroyed by Alien. He doesn't know any place he can go outside of NikeWorld because he's never left.

Falcon and Cheetah escape by following some lollipop arrows to Candy Crazy Clouds where they live happily ever after.

Meanwhile, Alien goes searching for Falcon in all of NikeWorld but, when he never finds Falcon, he gives up and decides to follow another prey. The prey he decides to catch is a hummingbird.

He's so concentrated on trying to catch the really fast hummingbird, he doesn't notice the NikeVolcano erupting NikeLava and he gets burned. He has to escape, and he follows the same lollipop arrows to Candy Crazy Clouds.

Because Candy Crazy Clouds is made of candy, he gives up looking for prey and just builds a house and lives happily ever after.

Samuel Medina is nine years old. He lives in Washington, DC. He had five fish, but three died. His fish died when he was seven years old. He is super strong, curious, smart, little, cute, and funny. He has a two-year-old brother. Samuel believes you should follow your heart.

Tree Tree's Life

written by Aleyah Garcia-Flores
illustrated by Sandra Maxa

Tree Tree was a girl tree who lived in a park. She liked to eat the nutrients in dirt, and her hair was made of leaves. She was ten years old. She liked animals and people and other trees, but she didn't have many friends.

She was so far from the other trees, except for a bully tree named BJ. BJ was eleven years old and he loved bullying Tree Tree. BJ bullied Tree Tree when his father wasn't looking. When BJ made fun of her, she cried.

One day, Tree Tree found a puppy. She called it Emma. Since Tree Tree got a puppy, BJ was jealous. BJ wanted to bully Tree Tree because he was so jealous.

Just as BJ was approaching Tree Tree, his father started calling him. BJ didn't hear his father, and kept bullying her. His father turned around and caught BJ bullying Tree Tree.

His father went up to Tree Tree and apologized on BJ's behalf. BJ got in trouble and was put in time out!

His father asked Tree Tree exactly what happened. Tree Tree said that BJ had been bullying her so badly that she started dreaming about BJ bullying her. When she awoke from that dream, she saw Emma. BJ's father was very sad about his son's bullying, so he said, "Let me make Emma something!" He made Emma a sweater, and that made Tree Tree very happy.

....

Aleyah Garcia-Flores is nine years old. She likes to play with Ashley, her younger sister. She has a puppy named Sophia. She loves her family. Her favorite movies are about puppies.

THE PROBLEM THAT HAS BEEN SOLVED

written by Bemnet Workneh Lobedo
illustrated by Emily Salinas

One day at Daffodil School, which goes from Pre-K all the way to twelfth grade, there were two flowers named Arizona and Torture. They were in seventh grade.

Arizona was mean, rude, ugly, loud, and had a bad attitude. Torture was not nice, very rude, and a bad girl.

And there were two nice daffodils named Sofia and Gift. It is important to know that Arizona and Sofia used to be old friends. Sofia and Gift were in sixth grade. Sofia was a not rude and a beautiful girl. Gift was the same as Sofia.

The first day of Daffodil School, Sofia and Gift became friends. One day at school, Arizona and Torture said, "Oh, you have other friends now? I thought Sofia was my friend." And then Torture started bullying Gift.

Arizona pushed Sofia into her locker because she had another friend. Torture was watching her and laughing. Arizona and Torture said, "If you tell the teacher on us, we'll hurt you even more."

Sofia and Gift whispered in each other's ear, "We can't just be bullied every time, every day. We have to tell the teacher."

But they didn't tell the teacher. They were still scared. It hurt them a lot to be in the locker because it was so small.

Gift told Sofia, "My mommy told me we shouldn't be scared of anything. No matter if somebody bullies you or tells you they're going to hurt you, you shouldn't be scared at all."

Sofia said, "We gotta do it. No matter

what, we have to tell the teacher."

They went to tell their teacher, Ms. Parrot, the math teacher. Arizona and Torture were in math class. Gift didn't know they were in math class, but she and Sofia went to math class and told Ms. Parrot about the bullying.

Ms. Parrot said, "Arizona and Torture! Why are you bullying them? That is so disrespectful. You girls are going to go to detention for one month."

After that, Arizona and Torture stopped bullying and Sofia and Gift lived happily ever after.

Bemnet Workneh Lobedo is a girl. She was born in DC. She is pretty like Mommy. She is also kind. Her full name is Bemnet Workneh Lobedo. She was born on May 21. She loves makeup. Bemnet is eight years old. She loves YouTube.

THE COCONUT TREES

written by Anthony Hernandez
illustrated by Halsey Berryman

Anthony and Tony are small coconut trees and they have lots of coconuts. They feel very cold because they live in a cold forest. Their coconuts fall off because they're so cold, they're shaking. The coconut trees want to move to New York because they think it's warm there.

Their friend is a person who lives in a clean house in New York. His name is Moises. He says, "Come in my house." He makes chicken soup for them to get warm.

Then Anthony and Tony stay in their friend's house. They don't go back to the forest because it's too cold there, and they belong in a warmer climate. They live in their friend's house forever because they like his warm house and his little dog named Rocky.

Anthony Hernandez is eight years old. He likes to play with his toy trucks. His favorite movie is *Teen Titans Go! To The Movies.* His favorite sport is football. In the future, he wants to be a chef.

69

DINO, SHARK, KRAKEN, AND EGG

written by Alexander Gregory Odett
illustrated by Alexander Oshiro

Mosasaurus and Spinosaurus are playing volleyball with a Megalodon egg. But the Megalodon sees they are playing with his egg. He calls some sharks over for backup.

Mosasaurus sees the sharks and says, "Yum, thanks for the snack!"

Megalodon gapes at Mosasaurus, "Did you just eat the sharks?!"

Spinosaurus says, "What? You haven't heard of the food chain? Unless you have friends bigger than a shark, you'll never get your egg back!"

"Okay," says the Megalodon. "I'll give you a Kraken to play with."

The Spinosaurus uses a spell and teleports the egg one hundred feet up.

"Look up there!" he says to the Megalodon.

The Megalodon sees the egg and says, "AHH! What do I do?"

Spinosaurus says, sarcastically, "I don't know? What do you do when you have a friend with tentacles longer than an anaconda?"

The Kraken reaches up to grab the egg with all of his tentacles and the egg falls into his tentacles five seconds later.

The Spinosaurus uses magic to glue the egg to Megalodon. "Now leave because I didn't know you had a friend who was a Kraken!"

Alexander Gregory Odett likes pets, fantasy, and video games. He is eight and has a cat named Macy who is one year old. He also has a dog named Linus who is 12 years old. He lives in Ft. Totten with his pets, parents, and brother. He dislikes bugs. Sometimes his imagination gets the better of him. He also gets annoyed easily, so don't annoy him! He's a Cerberus and a guard. (The guard part was sort of true, but the rest of that sentence was false.)

The Three Pigs in the Beautiful Forest

written by Josue Salaya Marquina
illustrated by Christina Girardi

The beautiful forest did not have a name. There were flowers in the forest, and the Three Pigs lived there.

The Three Pigs saw the wolf. They felt worried and scared because the wolf probably wanted to eat them.

They needed to make houses to stay safe, so each pig made their own house.

The wolf knocked down the door of the first house and blew it down.

The first pig ran to the second house.

The wolf knocked at the second house. Then he blew the house down. The two pigs ran to the third house, and the house was made of stone.

The wolf knocked on the door, then he blew...but it wouldn't fall down! The wolf went to the roof to get in through the chimney, but there was a fire in the chimney so he ran away.

The pigs were happy. The End.

Josue Salaya Marquina is a nine-year-old who lives in Washington, DC. His favorite movie is *The Flash*. He enjoys learning math. His dog's name is Gus and his cat's name is Sam. Josue and his little brother go to the same school.

PORTRAIT OF A TREE

written by Timothy Parks
illustrated by Teresa Roberts Logan

City Tree or Forest Tree?: City Tree

Name of Tree: Lol Tree

Favorite Activities: Running and jumping, relaxing

Least Favorite Activity: Being ignored

Describe the Perfect Day for Lol Tree: Saturday, Monday, Wednesday, Friday, and Sunday

What Would Happen on a Nice Saturday: Sun comes up. Wake up.

Typical Breakfast for Lol Tree: Rain, but not snow. Sunbeams. If they eat snow they will be frozen forever.

Typical Afternoon for Lol Tree: Eat lunch. Eat leaves.

Common Activities After Lunch: Eat dinner. Eat leaf-beans and sandwiches. That's it. And burgers.

Ways an Lol Tree Has Fun: Relaxes, sits down, lays on the grass

Dangers for an Lol Tree: There are hunter trees and trees can get hunted. Some get pickaxed by humans.

Ways an Lol Tree Spends its Birthday: November 23, 2001. It has a tree party.

Attendees of the Tree Party: Ophjoe comes to the tree party. The cards of queens. Kings of crowns. Halfjoe1235 (Ophjoe's brother). Ophio (born 2/8/2000).

Birthday Party Activities: At the birthday party they play Fortnite, Cars 3, Driftin to Win, and Cars 2.

Tree Snacks at the Party: Fruit snacks, chocolate cake, fruit cake, leaf cake, upside down pineapple cupcakes

Timothy Parks is an eight-year-old from Washington, DC. He is the middle child with one older sister and one younger sister. His family has a cat by the name of Fanta. If you catch him eating a snack, it'll most likely be a Pop-Tart.

BULLIES

written by Sythel Aquina Wandag
illustrated by Caitlin Cali

Once upon a time, there was a couple. The mother and the father had a daughter and a son! Their names were Mac and Gabrel. Mac was a girl.

The mother said, "When you grow up, you will be a warrior just like your father."

Mac said, "So we practice?"

Mom said, "Yes."

Gabrel said to Mac, "Always practice everyday."

Mac was six years old and Gabrel was eight years old. Mac didn't like to work, but Gabrel liked work, and practiced more and more. Mac liked to play with games and toys.

Gabrel was a brave boy, and Mac was scared of other people. She didn't like to see her brother hurt because she might cry if she did.

If Gabrel got hurt, he always said, "I'm fine," or, "I'm okay," and Mac would say, "Okay." Mac would hug him, and if Gabrel said, "That's enough now. You're squeezing me."

One day, Gabrel was playing soccer. He was looking for more people to play with him. There was a bully whose name was Jane. Mac and Gabrel were playing in her field, and she yelled at them to get off her field.

Gabrel didn't care about what Jane said. "This is not your field. This is everyone's!"

"Yeah, you're right," Jane said.

Mac agreed with what her brother said to the bully.

Never give up when a bully does something to you.

Sythel Aquina Wandag loves ice cream, like halo-halo. She is from the Philippines. Sythel loves to watch anime.

77

THE GREEDY LUMBERJACK

written by Dammien Wood
illustrated by Caitlin Saharek

Once upon a time, a lumberjack cut down mostly all the trees in a rainforest. He wanted to win a medal for cutting down 500 million trees.

There was a special healing tree that could heal you forever in the rainforest. When the lumberjack saw the prize for cutting down the special healing tree was $500 million, he decided to try.

The lumberjack found the tree. He noticed there were a lot of plants growing around it. Some of these plants were growing to be trees one day.

Anyway, the lumberjack tried to cut the tree. When the tree was cut halfway down, the plants around the tree grabbed the lumberjack and held him there.

The healing tree was thinking the whole time. The tree knew if it fell over to save the rest of the plants from getting cut, the tree would die. So the special tree fell and saved the plants anyway. The plants were saved, and the lumberjack did not win $500 million.

....

Dammien Wood likes video games. His favorite movie is *The Lego Movie 2: The Second Part*. His age is nine, his favorite book is *The Cat in the Hat*, and his favorite subject is math. In the future, he wants to own a gaming PC, a gaming chair, and a mouse.

RUPUNZEL II

written by Sofia Randall
illustrated by Sid Champagne

Once upon a time, there was a kingdom called Sugarville. Nobody knew where it was...well, except the queen, Rapunzel. But a mad scientist wanted to find it and take all the candy.

The Queen Rupunzel, of course, knew about this. She warned her people and candy animals. The mad scientist didn't stop looking for Sugarville until one day he bumped into the magical dark wall

portal that led to Sugarville.

When he got to Sugarville, there were bright cotton candy clouds, gummy birds, and everything was candy except the people.

When the citizens of Sugarville got the warning that the mad scientist was there, birds flew away, and hippos and elephants hid.

Since everything was hiding and he couldn't find any candy, the mad scientist got annoyed and left.

Queen Rupunzel and the citizens of Sugarville lived happily ever after.

Sofia Randall is eight years old. She likes playing basketball and soccer. When Sofia grows up, she wants to be a therapist. She lives in Washington, DC. She loves Easter because she goes on egg hunts. Also, her birthday is April 25. Also her favorite store is Claire's. Also she's very kind.

STINKEY AND THE ROSE

written by Heran Zelalem
illustrated by Eileen Chong

Stinkey really wants to be respected.

Stinkey was frustrated because he is jealous of Red Rose because she smells nice. One day Red Rose was talking to Stinkey. Red Rose saw that Stinkey was upset. "What's the matter?" she asked.

"I'm upset because nobody respects me," cried Stinkey. "Nobody will respect me, except for you."

"You are a corpse flower. You are supposed to stink. It's nothing to be upset about," said Red Rose.

"But I'm the only corpse flower in the jungle," said Stinkey.

"Why do you say you're the only corpse flower? What about your parents?" Red Rose asked.

"My parents died, so I'm the only Corpse Flower left," said Stinkey.

Red Rose said, "What about in a different part of the jungle?"

Heran Zelalem is eight years old. Her favorite thing to do is play *Roblox*. Heran was born in 2010. Her favorite movie is *The Grinch*.

"That may work! But we are rooted to the ground," said Stinkey.

A few days later, their roots got loose, so they pulled their roots out of the ground. Stinkey and Red Rose started to look for more Corpse Flowers. They searched all day and all night. But they didn't find anything.

But then they looked in a different part of the rainforest, and found a skunk. They didn't know what a skunk was but it stunk, so Stinkey was happy.

Plant City

written by Hienos Tekeste
illustrated by Alexander Oshiro

Chapter 1

A weeping willow named Rod loved the fresh air. One day, people came from all over town to hear the mayor speak an announcement. Even PlantSaver came flying up in the air, and animals came. Rod was so close that he could hear the mayor speak.

The mayor told everyone to take care of the trees and the park. "Don't step on the grass. Pick up the poop of your animals. Most of all: have fun!" the mayor said.

Rod could only speak in his mind because he was a tree. If he could speak, he would tell people stuff about trees. The mayor said that people should protect the trees because they give us what we need, and Rod was happy when he said that.

The next day, Rod only saw one or two families who were helping in the park. They watered Rod.

Chapter 2

The next day Rod noticed that more people were coming to the park, but they didn't care about him or the other trees. One and two families were working hard to help the trees. They worked all day but people still threw things at the trees.

PlantSaver was in his lab sleeping. He didn't even notice what was happening to all the plants. When he woke up, everyone in his plant family was feeling ill. Rod was, too.

PlantSaver had an alert: At the park, trash is everywhere and the plants look ill.

PlantSaver said, "By tomorrow, I will save the plants...Wait a second! I am PlantSaver! I am acting like other people who are lazy and don't care about anything but themselves."

PlantSaver went to the park so quickly, almost as fast as the speed of sound. When he got to the park, he saw very long lines all around.

Chapter 3

PlantSaver went to the other side of the park and saw all the sick plants. He tried to pick up the trash, but it was so stinky. PlantSaver turned to Rod, and Rod said, "We trees won't take it anymore."

PlantSaver knew he was a superhero celebrity and that people loved his autograph. PlantSaver flew up and said, "People! Stop and help plants! If you help the plants, I will give you an autograph." Everyone listened, and helped. PlantSaver gave his autograph to everyone who helped.

At the end, the park was so clean that PlantSaver cried and thanked everyone who helped the plants.

Hienos Tekeste likes to play sports, and he likes to draw and do origami. He lives in Washington, DC, he is an artist, and he is eight years old. He has a lot of dreams. In one of those dreams, he is flying like Superman through Washington, DC.

Hienos has been a lot of places, like the waterpark, museum, blueberry patch, food store in the forest, and a waterfall. He likes to play videogames, like *Fortnite*.

GREG AND THE DUCK

written by Warren Dwayne Walker, Jr.
illustrated by Eileen Chong

Greg is cool and the duck is the coolest. Greg and the duck go places, like the playground and the movies.

Greg wants to make food for the duck because the duck is hungry and wants to eat. But the problem is that Greg and the duck are suddenly not friends anymore, and Greg is crying.

They are bothering each other, and it has to stop.

Greg and the duck decide they don't want to bother each other anymore, and they become friends forever again.

Warren Dwayne Walker, Jr.'s favorite things are going to the zoo, playing with his PlayStation, going to his cousin's house, and going to Chuck E. Cheese and Dave & Buster's. Warren's favorite sport is football.

In the end, Greg and the duck are friends because they are not bothering each other, and so they live happily ever after.

The End.

The Cacao Tree and the Kid

written by Abel Zegeye
illustrated by Teresa Roberts Logan

One day, Abel was walking in the forest. He saw a crying cacao tree, and he asked what was wrong.

The tree responded. It said, "My old cacaos keep on falling off every day, and it's making me sad. I don't like it."

Abel thought for a long time. Then he came up with an idea. He went back to his home and he grabbed some tape. Then, he taped the cacaos to the tree branches.

Sadly, the cacaos fell off. All of them fell off!

Abel went home sad that night. He had wanted to help the cacao tree. He ate dinner, did his homework, watched some TV, and then went to sleep.

In the middle of the night, something magic and special happened. In the morning, small cacaos were growing on the tree!

The tree was really happy, and Abel was happy. They both lived happily ever after!

Abel Zegeye is a kid who is nine years old at Bridges. Abel was born in DC. He loves school. His birthday is on October 30.

Summer Light

written by Wengel Markos
illustrated by Julia Gualtieri

Once upon a time, there were two girls and two boys named Isabell, Sofia, Jt, and Sam. They were very, very, very nice but poor. Also, they didn't have enough money to buy nice clothes and food.

They lived in Sugarville, which was magical and had candy everywhere. It was also hot sometimes and warm other time. They had food, but not good food. They had JUNK FOOD.

One day, Isabell, Sofia, Jt and Sam all went to the Candy Sugar Mall when something caught their eyes. It was the place they had been waiting to go all their lives: the toy store.

"I want a colorful toy shell!" said Isabell.

"I want a baby kitten!" said Sofia.

"I want a HUGE Nerf gun!" said Sam.

"I want a spinner!" said Jt.

Then they saw they didn't have enough money, so they got jobs.

After they worked, they got the things they wanted, plus good food, not from Sugarville.

The family got rich, and they lived happily ever after.

The End.

Wengel Markos lives in Washington, DC. She loves to draw and color anything. She wants to do gymnastics in the future. She is nine years old, and she has a mom, dad, brother, and grandma.

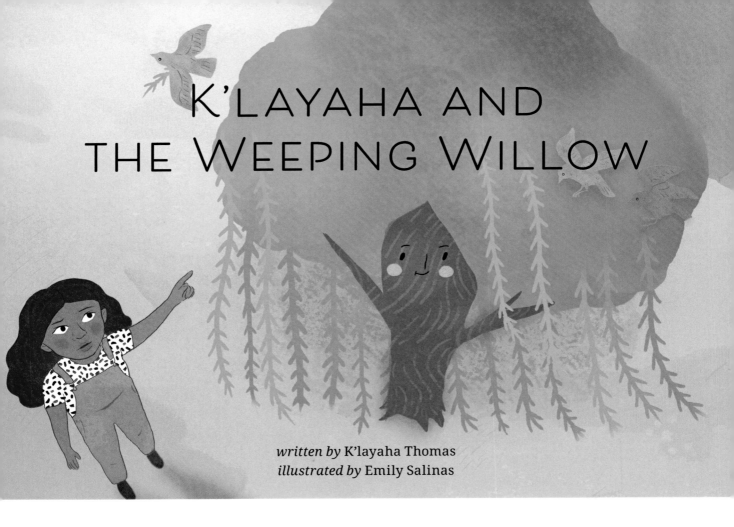

K'layaha and the Weeping Willow

written by K'layaha Thomas
illustrated by Emily Salinas

Once upon a time, there was a weeping willow named Kitty. Her best friend, K'layaha, was a regular girl.

Kitty and K'layaha had a problem. The birds kept on making a nest out of twigs and leaves, and K'layaha was worried they were going to take leaves and twigs from Kitty.

K'layaha said, "Kitty."

Kitty said, "Yes, K'layaha?"

"The birds are taking your leaves and twigs!" K'layaha said.

"It's okay. I like to share," said Kitty.

One day Kitty saw a boy weeping willow across the pond where she lived.

Kitty said, "Hi!"

"Do you want to have a picnic?" the boy weeping willow asked.

Kitty's branches and leaves froze in the wind.

K'layaha answered for Kitty. "Yes!"

"My name is Junior Moo, but I hate being called Moo because it is a funny name!" said Junior. Junior is nineteen years old.

The pond was the right place to have the picnic. Junior said, "We have sandwiches, peanut butter, jam, pear jam, a blanket, and pond water."

K'layaha, Kitty, and Junior lived happily ever after.

K'layaha Thomas is nine years old and she lives in Washington, DC. She is so into cats. Her favorite thing is a cat because cats are so cute and tiny—furry and fluffy, too.

THE JUNGLE STORY

written by Freddy Zelaya
illustrated by Sandra Maxa

This story starts in the jungle.

Boe is mean but happy. While in the jungle, he sees a flower he likes and calls it Sassy. It's a rose.

He looks around the jungle and sees bees. He has an idea. He gets honey to lure the mean bees away from him because he does not like bees.

He goes to his home and brings honey for the bees to eat. Then he sees Sassy, and he remembers something.

He takes the honey back and tells the bees to go to Sassy and eat her nectar. Then, the bees will spread pollen to make more roses for Boe and Sassy to be friends with!

Freddy Zelaya is a student. He is from El Salvador. He loves ice cream. He is funny. He loves dogs. He loves his family. He plays on his iPad. He is good at soccer. He loves to play with his dog. He plays with his dad.

IN THE CLOUDS

written by Ursula Adeline Mahoney Dingee
illustrated by Gigi Mascarenas

CHAPTER 1

Hi! My name is Kate, and I am a willow tree. I live near a pond by the main road of the city of Chitagaza. Chitagaza is a very floral place.

So, I was wondering if you could help me.

You can? Great!

So, my problem is that the clouds won't rain. I tried to ask them to make it rain, but they can't hear me! I need help making something to make them hear me!

I have tried breaking off one of my hollow branches and yelling into it, but they still can't hear me.

Can you break off one of my hollow branches, climb to the very top of my branches, and yell, 'Clouds, please make it rain!'"

You think about it for a long, long, long time. Finally, you decide to help, though you are puzzled by how you can talk to a tree. But you do what Kate said. You break off a branch and climb to the top of Kate. Then you yell into the branch, and say what Kate said to say, but the clouds do not hear you.

You climb back down and tell Kate the bad news.

CHAPTER 2

You tell Kate, "I am going to go home to get a bungee cord and some yellow string. I will be back in a few!"

So you run down your street. A few minutes later (about ten) you come back with what you said you would have. Then, you get two hollow branches and tie them together, and you yell up to the clouds.

THIS TIME THEY HEAR YOU!

They say, "We will rain every other Monday!"

The End.

....

Ursula Adeline Mahoney Dingee likes going roller skating. Her favorite color is blue. She likes french fries. Her birthday is March 18. Ursula's favorite drink is water.

Meet the Contributors

Darian
Amaya Robles

Mathias Beard

Malik Damar
Blackwell

Chase Brown

Brooklyn Michelle
DeChabert

Josiah Eury

Tomas Fita

Anna Flowers

Josiah French

Emmanuel
Fuentes-Ardon

Genesis
Fuentes-Ramirez

Aleyah
Garcia-Flores

Lauren Goganious

Akhil Hart

Jehison
Hernandez-Canales

Anthony Hernandez

Kaliyah Howard

Sierra Amber Howard

Destinee Jones

Joe'L Lawrence

Kayden Lee

Bemnet Workneh Lodebo

Ursula Adeline Mahoney Dingee

Wengel Markos

Bryson McCoy

Samuel Medina

Marcus Novoa

Alexander Gregory Odett

Manea Oulare

Timothy Parks

Genesis
Perez Salvador

Angel
Quinde Torres

Sofia Randall

Ariel Rodriguez
Beltran

Josue Salaya
Marquina

Wuan Shields

Landon Slade

Tyler Stewart

Sebastian
Stone Perea

Hienos Tekeste

K'layaha Thomas

Jayden Trice

Ephratah Tsegaye

Josue
Turcios-Salmeron

Marjorie
Valladares-Vera

Warren Dwayne Walker, Jr.   Sythel Aquina Wandag   Jervon Watson   Cameron Wise   Dammien Wood

Abel Zegeye   Heran Zelalem   Freddy Zelaya

Annie Wheeler is a digital communications specialist and photographer living and working in Washington, DC. When she's not trying to make people laugh for photos, she enjoys cooking, spending time outdoors, and learning about UX design. She can be reached at annie.wheeler46@gmail.com.

MEET THE ILLUSTRATORS

Patricia Baca is a designer, illustrator, and children's art educator. She was born in Mexico City, schooled in Kiev and Baltimore, and currently lives in DC with her husband and five-year-old son. She recently created MangoStreet, a Neighborhood Imaginarium for children. She can be contacted at patricia@patriciadesigns.live, mangostreetdc.com, and on Instagram at @mangostreetdc.

Halsey Berryman is a designer and illustrator born, raised, and based in Washington DC. She is a graduate of the Corcoran College of Art and Design, where she earned her BFA in painting and fine arts. Halsey is a multidisciplinary designer who works in custom typography, digital illustration, murals, and more. Newcolumbiasigns@Gmail.com; (978) 621 6055.

Caitlin Cali is an artist living in Providence, RI. She makes bright, playful and emotive drawings and paintings with the hope that her work will leave people feeling less alone. See her work on her Instagram page: @caitlin.m.cali.

Santiago Casares is an author/illustrator originally from Mexico City. He's the creator of *Chili's World*, *Lunatic Tales*, and *Nursery Rhymes Comics*. You can see his portfolio at the aptly named santiagocasares.com.

Sid Champagne lives in Baltimore with their cat, Jonathan. They work in a library and spend their free time baking, singing, and drawing. You can find more info on Sid at sidchampagne.com.

Eileen Chong is a visual and literary storyteller grown in the Midwest but now rooted in DC. Her work can be found at www.thespiderplant.com.

Samantha Lane Fiddy is a freelance artist, author, and mom to three sweet kids. She lives in a home full of LEGOS and unicorns in Falls Church, VA, and loves collaborating with 826DC. You can view her full portfolio at samanthalanefiddy.com and follow her sketchbook adventures on Instagram at @samanthalanefiddy.

Christina Girardi is a fine artist based in the Washington, DC metro area whose work focuses on portraiture and landscapes. Her approach incorporates the freshness of direct observation from life, with a unique perspective that inspires new ways of looking. She can be reached at contact@christinagirardi.com, or at her website, christinagirardi.com.

Julia Gualtieri draws, makes books, and prints. She also teaches children, teens, and college students. She likes mangos. She can be reached at juliagualtieri.com.

Kendall Ladd is an arts advocate, grant writer, and illustrator in Washington, DC. Her work is whimsical, a bit surreal, and often involves dinosaurs. She can be reached at kendall.ladd@gmail.com.

Teresa Roberts Logan is a comic storyteller, a syndicated and Reuben-nominated cartoonist, and a regular contributor to DC's *Magic Bullet* comics newspaper and Dirty Diamonds All-Girl Comics Anthology, as well as Vagabond Comics and Cartoonists Draw Blood's *Trick Or Treat*. Her work has been featured in The Center for Cartoon Studies' *Cartoon Crier*, and her *Laughing Redhead Comics* appear at GoComics.com. She makes regular appearances at ComicCons, Zine Fairs, and on various stages, selling her comedy, comics, and cartoons. Her website is LaughingRedhead.com. Her Twitter and Instagram are @LaughingRedhead.

Gigi Mascarenas is a Chicago-raised queer Filipina visual and performance-based storyteller. She embraces storytelling as a medium to connect individuals and spark dialogue, including the use of design to bring stories to visual life. Gigi loves to support her favorite community spaces, greets plants, and hangs out with her niece-cat, Molly.

Sandra Maxa works as an illustrator, designer and partner at Q Collective, a multi-disciplinary studio in Baltimore that creates identity, interactive, environmental and book projects for (mostly) nonprofit clients. She also teaches at Maryland Institute College of Art where she directs the Graphic Design Master of Arts program. Get in touch at sandie@upwithq.com.

George Nichols IV is a graphic designer and illustrator. George's approach to work is always fun, personal, and draws from his diverse professional and cultural background. His goal is to serve as a catalyst for cultural impact in the design community. He can be reached at his website, georgenicholsiv.com, or via email at gniv1507@gmail.com.

Alexander Oshiro is an illustrator, video editor, and motion graphics designer who was born in LA like, once, and won't let it go. He lives in Silver Spring, Maryland, loves coffee, cooking, and culture, and has very strong opinions on anime and dragons. He can be found on Instagram at @oshiroalexander, or online at oshiroalexander.com.

Leslie Osmont is professional graphic designer and illustrator living in Baltimore MD. She's had a love and talent for the arts for as long as she can remember. She pulls much of her inspiration from the weird and wonderful natural occurrences all around us. She believes we see magic everyday when the sun rises and she hopes to make observers see the mundane as magical through her work. Contact Leslie for illustration or design work at leslieosmont@gmail.com, through her Etsy shop etsy.com/shop/lozluna or via her website losmontdesign.com.

Max Reinhard is a mixed media interdisciplinary artist who utilizes a range of materials including gouache, acrylic, graphite, digital, and more. His technical approach is often graphic and illustrative, but can also deviate to a more realistic or even abstract application. Capturing mood through use of color is paramount in his practice, as is the exploration of shape and dynamic lighting. Reinhard builds his artistic practice primarily through plein air painting and illustrative drawing. Painting from life informs Reinhard's treatment of light, shape, and color, where illustrative drawing provides the concept, line, and flow. Reinhard can be reached through his website, rhine-art.com.

Caitlin Saharek is a graduate of the Rhode Island School of Design and works as an artist and designer out of Providence, Rhode Island. Her work ranges from wayfinding and map design to murals to tiny intricate dioramas. Send a hello to caitlinsaharek@gmail.com.

Emily Salinas is an illustrator and designer based in Baltimore. Originally from the South, she draws upon her love of everyday eclecticism and illustrates using painterly layers in a vivid color palette. When she isn't doodling, you can find her at home in the kitchen or playing music with friends.

Acknowledgements

A million, billion, gazillion thanks to the young authors of this book. We are so grateful for the chance to meet them and hear their stories. This book would not be here without their hard work, delightful imaginations, and, most importantly, their voices.

We need just as many thanks to express our appreciation for our partners at Bridges Public Charter School. Kristin Anclien, Audrey Childs, Jenny Fernandez, Conal O'Keefe, Virginia O'Rourke, Brittany Seldon, and Aurelio Valentine welcomed us into their classrooms and supported the book from the beginning.

Many thanks to the volunteers—Steven Blume, Tara Campbell, David Garfinkel, Vince Granata, and Rachel Kanter—who served as mentors for the writers. Their energy, flexibility, consistency, and care were the bedrock of this book. Special thanks to Tara Campbell and Lauren Johnson—they volunteered as visiting artists, shared their work with the writers, and led workshops on character voice and on setting, important elements in many of these stories.

We owe a special thank you to two of our partners in education. To Tiffany McGettigan and the Hirshhorn Museum, thank you for providing a curated museum experience for our young authors. Thank you to Dr. Hollyn Karapetkova and her EN 270 Approaches to Creative Writing class at Marymount University for their copyediting support, and for all the snazzy fan mail.

Minh Lê wrote the foreword, the perfect beginning for this fearless book. We thank him for sharing his words and his optimism for the future. We definitely owe him a pack of Now and Laters.

This beautiful book wouldn't have been possible without a crew of creators. Annie Wheeler photographed the authors, and we thank her for the enthusiasm and care that went into capturing the unique spirit of each writer. We're incredibly grateful for the following illustrators for bringing each of these stories to life: Patricia Baca, Halsey Berryman, Caitlin Cali, Santiago Casares, Sid Champagne, Eileen Chong, Samantha Lane Fiddy, Christina Girardi, Julia Gualtieri, Kendall Ladd, Teresa Roberts Logan, Sandra Maxa, George Nichols IV, Alexander Oshiro, Leslie Osmont, Max Reinhard, Caitlin Saharek, and Emily Salinas. In the beginning, we dreamed of a book as vibrant and animated as the authors, and these illustrators went above and beyond our fledgling fantasies. Dave Kriebel also joined us in our vision for the design of the book and created promotional materials so beautiful that we are considering wallpapering our homes with the imagery.

Gigi Mascarenas is one of the many reasons this

project is a book and not just a bunch of Google Docs. She designed the book's layout, illustrated two stories, created the cover, and weighed in on many design choices. Storytelling is core to who she is and what she does, and it shows throughout this book. Gigi, a long-time friend of 826DC, deserves our boundless, heartfelt thanks.

As always, we are indebted to the staff members and interns at 826DC, whose hands have left indelible fingerprints on this, and on many other projects: Shayna Baggatts-Porter, Cedric Brown, Eileen Chong, Zachary Clark, Max Davidson, Jesse Eisenstein, D'Real Graham, Cris Lee, April Little, Kelsey McClure, Holly Moak, Areesah Mobley, Molly Reigert, Sarah Richman, and Brandi Shorts. The thoughtfulness and passion they bring to their work at 826DC can never be celebrated enough. These thanks are a small attempt at doing so, but we'll also bring cupcakes to the next staff meeting.

We offer our unending gratitude to Kennerley Roper, current intern and forever friend of 826DC, for the delicate care with which she approached every aspect of this book. Without her diligent thoughtfulness, we would not be publishing a book this May. Thank you.

One 826DC staff member, in particular, deserves her own shout-out. Emily Moses—editor extraordinaire, curriculum genius, logistical gymnast, and literary mastermind—spent hundreds of hours and hundreds of pink sticky notes to bring this book into being.

Just as no person is an island, no book is a solitary feat. We would also like to thank our many marvelous partners for their generous support in this collaboration: Catherine Wakelyn (in honor of Emory T. Carl), Joe and Nell Callahan, Rita O'Donnell and Alan Bergamini, Leif and Julia Ulstrup, Tara Greco, Jenna Howard, Ray Kimsey, David Pryor, Jr., Eric Schwerin, Amy Tejral, David Wakelyn, the DC Commission on the Arts and Humanities, the Morris and Gwendolyn Cafritz Foundation, the Harman Family Foundation, the International Paper Foundation, the Kimsey Foundation, the Jack Kent Cooke Foundation, the Lannan Center for Poetics and Social Practice at Georgetown University, the Share Fund, the Elkes Foundation, the Lainoff Family Foundation, Washington REIT, Charlotte Witherspoon and Cornerstone Research, 826 National, the 826DC Board of Directors, and the 826DC Programs Committee, specifically Ron Charles, Amy Pastan, Dr. Miah Daughtery, and W. Ralph Eubanks.

We hope that this book will be a source of pride and a beacon of hope for everyone involved.